WANTED

The most EVIL WICKED ABHORRENT VILE villain to ever curse this world . . . or any other.

VILLAINS

THE EVILEST
OF THEM ALL

studio **fun**
INTERNATIONAL

Evil Queen

SKILLS:
- Disguises
- Poisons
- Curses
- Wicked plots
- Enchantment and general sorcery

PRIZED POSSESSION:
- Magic Mirror

EDUCATION:
- Studied alchemy, transmogrification, and advanced hexes at ████████ Academy of Black Magic

PRIOR WORK EXPERIENCE:
- Several years as monarch of ████████ (currently deposed)
- Sorceress of repute throughout the surrounding lands and kingdoms
- Fairest in the land

HAIR COLOR:
- Raven black

EYE COLOR:
- Toxic green

Magic Mirror, on the wall, who is <u>MOST</u> villainous of them all?

Thy deeds are certainly evil, my queen, but most villainous . . . such a judgment may be beyond even my great powers. I believe there may be those who surpass even thee.

A highly suspect assumption. Allow me to recall a certain tale, the ending of which will make one's blood run as cold as ice.

Chilling thy tale may be my queen, but I have no blood to frost, nor veins to freeze.

You are far too literal-minded, Mirror. It is an expression, nothing more! Now be silent, and listen to my story.

<u>ONCE UPON A TIME,</u> I was the ruler of a large and prosperous kingdom. Not only was I queen of all that I surveyed, but all who beheld me could not help but agree that I was the **FAIREST** and **MOST BEAUTIFUL** creature in all the land.

I was both loved and feared—none dared disobey my every wish and whim. I was even able to make my own stepdaughter, Snow White, into a lowly serving maid.

But one accursed day I was told that my status as the fairest was . . . in question. Indeed, it was Snow White herself who had usurped my place.

 Indeed. It was I who informed you of this fact.

 Yes, and if I did not value you so, I would have taken a stone and dashed you to pieces on the spot!

And yet, such an insult could not stand. So I called a huntsman to my throne room, and ordered him to take Snow White into the forest and to do away with her. As proof, I requested that he return to me with her heart encased in a jeweled box.

A *truly heartless decision, my queen.*

Do NOT patronize me.

Of course the fool bungled the job, and his incompetence forced me to take matters into my own hands. With my mastery of the dark arts, I disguised myself as a humble apple peddler, and crafted an apple which was poisoned with the draught of Sleeping Death. One bite of the apple would send her into a sleep so deep that nothing could awaken her.

 Except true love's first kiss.

What? Nonsense. Who would leave such an obvious loophole in a perfectly good evil spell? You must be misremembering. Now quiet, lest I fetch that stone I spoke of.

 Yes, my queen.

I made my way deep into the forest where the girl was hiding. She had taken refuge with some forest-dwelling dwarfs, but I cleverly arrived while they were away. I persuaded her to take a bite of the apple. I told her it granted wishes, the silly little simpleton! She fell to the floor, never to wake again. Once more, I was THE FAIREST IN THE LAND!

 . . . Is that all?

 OF COURSE THAT'S ALL.

I seem to recall that Snow White was, indeed, awoken by true love's first kiss, and you were defeated by woodland creatures, my queen.

Madness! First this "true love's first kiss" nonsense! And now you believe that I, the fairest and evilest woman there ever was, would be defeated by a cadre of rabbits, birds, and deer? Have you taken leave of your senses, Mirror?

I suppose next you'll tell me that Snow White was awoken by a handsome prince, and they rode off together on his white horse to live happily ever after!

 *Well, actually~*

Magic Mirror, hear me well, this fairy tale is mine to tell. And I say that I AM THE <u>FAIREST</u>, and Snow White sleeps still! That is the true end of the story.

 Whatever you say, MY QUEEN.

SKILLS:

- Hypnotism
- Conjuring
- Crystal gazing
- Sorcery

EDUCATION:

- Learned magic from the ancient sands (self-taught)

PRIZED POSSESSION:

- Enchanted cobra staff

PRIOR WORK EXPERIENCE:

- All-powerful genie
- Royal Vizier to the Sultan of the Kingdom of Agrabah
    - Organized the dungeons to be more efficient
    - Oversaw quick executions of criminals
    - Brought back corporal punishment for thieves, vagabonds, and ruffians
    - Sultan of Agrabah

Yeah, for about five minutes.

LIKES:

- Infinite power
- Wealth beyond imagining
- Absolute obedience
- Humiliating enemies
- Scheming and conniving

HAIR COLOR:

- Dark as a sandstorm

EYE COLOR:

- Black as a starless sky

DISLIKES:

- Good-hearted thieves
- Meddling princesses
- Being a servant
- Being outsmarted
- Genies

Nine million, nine hundred eighty-four thousand, nine hundred and twenty-six jugs of water on the wall, nine million, nine hundred eighty-four thousand, nine hundred and twenty-five jugs of water—

Silence, Iago! *If I have to listen to one more chorus of that dratted song, I will glue your wretched beak shut!*

Oh yeah? And how exactly will you do that **Mr. Has-Been?**

I tell you, Iago, I am the most villainous villain there ever is or was. And the most powerful. I have infinite cosmic powers.

 Yeah, and you're stuck in a cramped lamp with me while that street-rat Aladdin lives the good life with his princessy-poo.

An unfortunate, and temporary situation. **Allow me** *to remind you.*

I rose through the ranks to become the Sultan of Agrabah's second-in-command. Of course, observing the man up close, it became clear to me how incompetent he was.

My ambitions would not allow me to stand idly by while such a fool ran the kingdom into the ground. I had to seize power by any means necessary. Agrabah deserved a sultan who had its "best interests" at heart. MY INTERESTS.

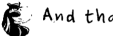 And that was you.

OF COURSE IT WAS ME!

My staggering intellect allowed me to trace the location of a magical artifact—a genie's lamp. The power of a genie would be enough to grant the power, riches, and social position I desired. Unfortunately, it was hidden in a place that I could not access—the Cave of Wonders. Only a so-called "diamond in the rough" could enter.

It was just my bad luck that the "diamond" in question was that idiot boy, Aladdin.

Yeah, that punk threw a real monkey wrench in our plans.

MY PLANS, IAGO.

Y'know, I'm starting to feel pretty unappreciated here.

Aladdin stole the lamp which was ~~rightfully mine~~, and used it to make himself a prince, in order to woo the sultan's defiant daughter, Jasmine. It would have been laughable, had he not been directly interfering with my strategy to marry Jasmine

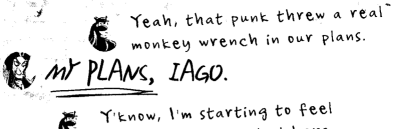

myself. I was so close to *hypnotizing* the Sultan into agreeing that she should be my wife, making me next in line for the throne, when that pretender prince arrived and ruined my chances.

Yeah, if you'd married Jasmine, we could have gotten papa-in-law out of the way. You'd have been on the throne, **NO GENIE MAGIC REQUIRED.**

Ugh, don't remind me. Fortunately, once I realized the so-called prince was just a street rat, and that he must have the lamp with him somewhere, retrieving it was exceedingly simple. Using my genie wishes, I was able to get the princess, the Sultan, and Aladdin out of the way so that I could rule Agrabah with an iron fist.

Yeah, and then he got one over on you—AGAIN. The oldest trick in the book, too. "Nyah nyah, the Genie's more powerful than you!" He convinced you to wish to become a genie.

A simple miscalculation. Yes, I did wish to become a genie. And as I desired, I possessed infinite cosmic powers—powers that were unrivaled by any other being in the universe!

Yeah, and just like every genie, you also have a teeny-tiny lamp to live in and are forced to do the bidding of any schmuck who rubs you the wrong way.

And as if the torment of my imprisonment wasn't enough, I'm stuck with you. You loud-mouthed, insufferable, avian annoyance.

This isn't a picnic for me, pal! I don't even get genie powers! Why don't you do some magic and put me to sleep so I don't have to listen to your whining?

If I could perform any magic at all, I would have DESTROYED this lamp and freed us both ages ago! But mark my words, Iago. Someday I will find a way out of this servitude, and then I will once again be a villainous force to reckon with.

Mother Gothel

PRIOR WORK EXPERIENCE:

- Magician
- Tower architect
- Mercenary management
- ~~Crone~~

SKILLS:

- Magical botany
- Psychological manipulation
- Killer beauty routine:
    - Wash your face every morning and night with cold, clear water
    - Remember that sunlight prematurely ages the skin
    - Maintain a regular exercise regimen of climbing towers to keep fit
    - Brush your kidnapped daughter's magical hair with at least 100 strokes a day

WEAPON OF CHOICE:
- Dagger

EDUCATION:
- School of hard knocks

HAIR COLOR:
- ~~Old Crone Gray~~ Obsidian black

EYE COLOR:
- Stormy gray

LIKES:
- Unquestioning obedience
- Magical flora
- Eternal youth
- Being left alone

DISLIKES:
- Ungrateful children
- Nosy thieves
- Meddlesome royals
- Old age

Villain? Really, is it villainous to steal a girl away from her parents because she possesses the magic necessary to maintain your eternally youthful appearance?

YES. DEFINITELY.

You want me to be the bad guy? **FINE. I'M THE BAD GUY.** But really, that sundrop flower was rightfully mine. I found it first. Yes, yes, the queen was dying, and yes, I "stole the princess," but the real crime would be letting beauty like mine fade.

Besides, I was only trying to do what was best for Rapunzel. You think she would have been happy as a princess? All those responsibilities, all those people hanging around her, all that attention? Please!

I gave her a carefree life, locked away safe in a tower, free from all the horrors of the outside world. Her every need catered to by me! All I asked in return was for her to stay by my side forever and keep me eternally young. **THAT'S NOT TOO MUCH, IS IT?**

 UHH . . .

I thought not. I indulged her every whim. That girl has so many hobbies—sewing, painting, reading books, playing musical instruments, and singing, and, **MY GOODNESS**, the mumbling, but did I complain? No! Because a good mother loves her daughter despite her many, many flaws.

Despite the fact that she was awkward, ungainly, naïve, ditzy, immature, gullible, had no idea how to dress or bathe properly, and did I mention the constant teenage chattering—ugh!

Despite all that, I loved her. Unconditionally.

YOU SURE ABOUT THAT?

Oh, please, you're not a mother. You couldn't possibly understand.

Of course, to top it all off, the first chance she gets, Rapunzel runs off with Flynn Rider—a lowly thief. I certainly raised her better than that.

I was absolutely devastated when I came back to the tower and found her missing. I tore the place apart. When I found the crown, I feared something dreadful must have happened to her.

But no, she'd just run off with the first man she'd ever seen! All to see those silly lanterns. Just because they appeared on her birthday every year.

In hindsight, I never should have told her about birthdays. That would have saved me a headache.

HEY, PATCHY, ARE YOU STARTING TO THINK THIS LADY MIGHT BE A LITTLE OFF HER ROCKER?

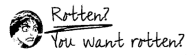

I can hear you, you know! Anyway, hiring you two to kidnap Rapunzel's little "boyfriend" Rider and trick her into returning to me was really all for her own good.

YEAH, AND THEN YOU BETRAYED US. YOU SOLD US OUT, JUST LIKE RIDER. WE ENDED UP IN THE CASTLE DUNGEONS WITH HIM!

Oh, who cares? The important thing is that I got what I wanted, even if I had to do a little backstabbing to get there. It's like I always told Rapunzel, you have to look out for number one— AND NUMBER ONE IS ALWAYS ME.

Rapunzel was back where she belonged—in the tower, with me. But then . . . ugh, she somehow remembered that she was actually a princess, and had the NERVE to claim that I wasn't her real mother! After I'd spent all those years martyring myself to that girl. I had to tie her up. It's what any mother would do.

I DON'T KNOW, LADY. THAT'S PRETTY ROTTEN, EVEN BY OUR STANDARDS.

Rotten?
You want rotten?

Rotten is betraying your own mother for a man you just met. Rotten is selfishly ignoring years of good advice to "follow your dreams." Rotten is allowing some ruffian to cut off your beautiful, magical, youth-restoring hair! After all I'd done for her . . . the ingratitude is almost enough to make you cry.

HEY! WE NEVER CRY! PATCHY HERE ONLY HAS ONE EYE, AND IT'S NEVER SHED A SINGLE TEAR!

Good for you, boys. Crying causes premature aging, you know. Unfortunately, so does destroying the source of the sundrop's power, apparently. All those years of carefully preserved beauty, ruined with one stroke of the knife!

And that's the story of how my wicked, ungrateful, self-centered daughter betrayed me and left me bereft and wronged and wrinkled. Anyone can see that I'm the injured party here. WHERE'S MY HAPPILY EVER AFTER, I ASK YOU?

Lady Tremaine

SKILLS:
- Household management
- Self-control
- Manipulation
- Social climbing

PRIOR WORK EXPERIENCE:
- Mother
- Homemaker

HOW TO KEEP YOUR HOUSE SPOTLESS:
- Enlist your least favorite daughter as a servant
- Pay her only in food and board
- Criticize everything she does to make her work harder
- Keep her busy every hour of every day to cut down on daydreaming and listlessness

EDUCATION:
- Only the finest finishing schools

PRIZED POSSESSION:
- Cane

HAIR COLOR:
- Dowager gray

EYE COLOR:
- Envious green

LIKES:
- Obedient children
- Propriety
- Increased social status
- Wealth
- Extravagance
- Lucifer, my beloved cat

DISLIKES:
- Selfish step-daughters
- Disobedience
- Poverty
- Embarrassment
- Mice

I have been called a wicked stepmother. Of course, any stepmother will tell you that wickedness seems to come with the territory; no matter what you do, it never seems good enough. I ask you, is it wickedness to wish for _perfection_ in all things?

Of course not, mother!

What happened to us is so unfair.

I couldn't agree more. After my husband, your stepfather, passed away, we were left practically destitute, and I was saddled with a stepdaughter, Cinderella, for my trouble. And I treated her with all the kindness I felt she deserved. After all, she was an _absolute nightmare_ of a girl always singing, and daydreaming, and making friends with pestilent creatures like bluebirds and mice. Her father had completely spoiled her!

She once put a mouse under my teacup!
Ohh, it was horrid!

I remember that! I could hear your
screeching all the way in my bedroom.
It was HILARIOUS-er, I mean, horrible.

Such a cruel joke to play on my darling daughter.
Remember, she even discouraged my sweet Lucifer
from chasing the little vermin?

MEOW!

I know, my pet. It was clear
that if she was left idle she'd
be up to no good. So, I did
what I must. I set her to
proper work—I had her sweeping,
mending, sewing, and washing
every second of every day to
keep her head out of the
clouds and based in reality.

It was all for her edification, really. ANY proper gentleman would prefer a cultured, practical girl like you two—not a drowsy dreamer like Cinderella.

Humph! You'd think so anyway!

All those years of elocution and voice lessons, *completely* wasted.

Well, how was I to know a fairy godmother would come along and spoil all my hard work? A wave of her wand undid all the discipline I'd spent years and years instilling in my stepdaughter. Not to mention all the years I'd spent advancing you two in society!

Mother, why don't we have fairy godmothers?

We DEMAND fairy godmothers! One for each of us!!

Right! I refuse to share!

Hush, girls. I was as shocked as you were when Cinderella appeared at the royal ball in all that finery. (I knew it was her, of course.) And then she had the gall to dance with the prince! As if she belonged there, among all those noble people.

Of course, I was even more shocked when the prince actually reciprocated her feelings.

He should have been mine!

You mean MINE

Don't fret. It was a sign of poor breeding on his part, I'm sure. He'll get tired of her soon enough. Or perhaps it was some kind of joke, or a dalliance . . .

MROW?

But they're married, mother.

Please, don't remind me. Just remember, girls: cream rises to the top. And we are certainly the cream of this family.

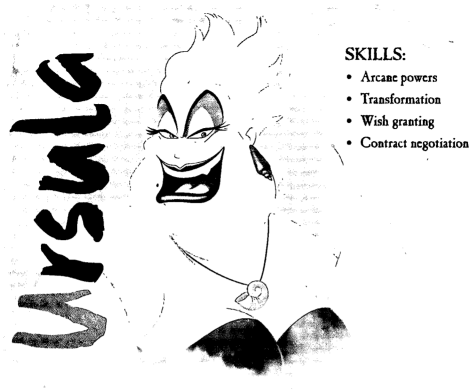

Ursula

SKILLS:
- Arcane powers
- Transformation
- Wish granting
- Contract negotiation

PRIOR WORK EXPERIENCE:
- Royal sorceress of Atlantica
- Freelance sea witch
- Queen of the seven seas (dethroned)

EDUCATION:
- No need for education when you have natural magical talents.

PRIZED POSSESSION:
- Triton's crown and trident

HAIR COLOR:

- Seafoam white

EYE COLOR:

- Blue as the sea in a storm

LIKES:

- Cauldrons and potions
- Palace life
- Adoration
- Righteous vengeance
- My sweet little poopsies, Flotsam and Jetsam
- Tending to my "garden"

DISLIKES:

- Banishment
- Back talk
- King Triton
- Meddling seagulls and mangy mongrels
- People who break legally and magically binding contracts

King Triton made a grave error when he banished me from his kingdom. Why, I have more WICKED WILES in the tip of my tentacle than the rest of the ocean dwellers put together. No one is more DEVILISH and DEVIOUS than Ursula! It was only a matter of time before I got my revenge on him and his whole blasted kingdom. But I'm a reasonable sea witch, aren't I, boys?

Very reasonable, Ursula!

. . . For a sea witch.

I let Triton tie his own noose. After all, if his kingdom were the underwater wonderland he pretended it was, my services wouldn't have been needed. But no, his citizens flocked to me for solutions to their problems. Me, not him! I used my mighty powers to help those in need, creating potions and magic to solve their every dilemma. And, if I helped myself too, well, that's just good business.

And the great and mighty King Triton was completely oblivious to my dealings. As though I'd meekly obey his orders! No, I lurked, and I planned. I consolidated my magic powers, and I bided my time, waiting for the moment that Triton was at his weakest.

I doubt he'd have even noticed if his own precious daughter hadn't come to me for help.

HA! What a stroke of luck that was! Princess Ariel desperately wanted something only I could deliver: two legs and a chance to meet and marry the human prince she'd fallen in love with. Just another poor, unfortunate soul I was driven to help.

A little encouragement got her to swim to my cave and strike a deal with me. And all I asked for in return was her voice. A perfectly equitable trade.

 Thoroughly generous.

 Very.

 It's not MY fault she couldn't close the deal.

Well . . . you did disguise yourself as a human too.

 And use magic to make Prince Eric fall in love with you.

Oh, come now. The contract never specified that I wouldn't interfere. Merfolk are so trusting.

Besides, Ariel and her prince weren't the ones I wanted. It was nothing personal, honestly. I had much bigger fish to fry---King Triton was always the real target.

He was the one who banished me from Atlantica and forced me to live in exile, wasting away, forgotten and practically starving! I had to pay him back for my years of misery. To do so, I'd have to be more powerful than he was.

And with his daughter in my grasp, I knew that Triton would do whatever I wanted. I only had to ask.

So, I had him sign a contract. **Ha!**

He was only too happy to trade his own life away in return for his dear Ariel's safety, just as I had planned. He withered away into a polyp, and I was free to pick up his trident and his crown. My villainous scheme was right on track.

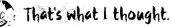

And with the power of his trident, the ocean was mine to command! The seas bowed to my power! I could call lightning from the sky, summon storms, and create whirlpools with a wave of my hand.

And then . . . well, I simply decided that ruling the ocean wasn't for me. I have much, much bigger fish to fry these days. And I don't care what you think you heard—I certainly was NOT defeated by Ariel's little human princeling.

Right?!??

 Definitely not.

 Never happened, Ursula.

That's what I thought.

PRIOR WORK EXPERIENCE:

- Leader of the hyenas
- Ruler of the Pride Lands

EDUCATION:

- Only my natural cunning

SKILLS:

- Natural leadership
- Superior intelligence
- Strategic planning
- Discipline
- Manipulation

WEAPON OF CHOICE:

- Claws and teeth

EYE COLOR:

- Savanna yellow

MANE COLOR:

- Midnight black

LIKES:

- Unquestioned authority
- Taunting helpless foes
- Ruling the Pride Lands

DISLIKES:

- The so-called "Circle of Life"
- Exile
- Elephant Graveyard
- Being blamed
- Smart-mouthed lionesses
- Uppity nephews

Ever since my brother Mufasa was chosen over me to rule the Pride Lands, I knew that I would have to fight and CLAW MY WAY TO THE TOP on my own. It should have been clear to everyone from day one that I was the rightful heir to the throne. Instead, I spent my entire cub-hood playing second fiddle to my "dear" brother, who was given every privilege, every consideration. Well, Mufasa may have gotten the brawn, but I got the lion's share of the brains.

You said it, boss!

Right, boss!

Oooooh! Heheheehee!

Unfortunately, brute strength isn't so easy to overcome. Certainly, it would be simple to outwit my brother, but how could I do it so that he was removed from the equation without any suspicion falling upon me?

Then, while *I* was weighing my options, biding my time, my wretched brother had a cub of his own. And of course, the moment my nephew Simba was born, everyone was falling all over themselves for the "FUTURE KING." But Simba was just another lion standing between me and the throne. *I* quickly realized *I*'d have to bare my teeth and my ambitions—before the wretched little brat grew up and caused me even more problems.

I thought at least Simba would be easy to take care of. *I* lured him and his little friend Nala to the Elephant's Graveyard, where you three were lying in wait. Two lion cubs should have been a piece of cake for you.

AooouughL!
Eeeeek!
Hahaha!

Mufasa showed
up before we could lay a
claw on them. Even three to one, we couldn't take
him down.

Well, perhaps if you'd spent less time making jokes and more time DOING YOUR JOBS!

No matter. Your failure revealed to me the flaws in my plan to kill Simba and Mufasa and take the throne. If I tried to kill Simba alone, Mufasa would come to his aid and save them both. And I realized the lionesses would make Mufasa all but impossible to get to.

So I devised a different, but cunning plan to become King. I got Simba to the bottom of the canyon, then ran to tell my dear brother that his precious son was in mortal peril. You and your hyena friends started a stampede of wildebeest, right through where Simba would be waiting.

 Yeah, killing Mufasa by setting up a stampede in the canyon was a brilliant idea, boss.

 It had every earmark of a TRAGIC ACCIDENT. Exactly as I'd planned.

 Like we planned. We helped, too.

Indeed, you did. And what's a little regicide between friends?

You're one vicious guy, Scar.

Unquestionably. And it all went off without a hitch—except for one thing. My darling nephew didn't perish in the stampede. So I left it to you three imbeciles to get him out of the picture.

Hey, we did get him out of the picture! We just didn't kill him.

That's what "out of the picture" means, you IDIOTS. You failed at the simplest part of the very simple task I'd set. I suppose this is what I get for trusting hyenas with my dirty work.

At least since I'd told Simba that his father's death was his fault—a brilliant bit of improvisation if I do say so myself—he believed me and exiled himself. I had the Pride Lands under my claw for the time being. Once I told the lionesses that Mufasa and Simba were dead, it was easy enough to slip into my natural role as ruler.

At last, I was taking what was owed to me . . . . what *I* deserved!

 And you did keep your promises to us.

 Yeah, you let us into the Pride Lands where we could eat all we wanted. Livin' the high life. The lion life.

 Eeeehehehehe!

Yes . . . that may have been one of my RARE errors.

Hey!

It's not our fault you were a terrible king!

I was a magnificent king. Your folly and ravenous appetites are wholly to blame for what happened next. You ate the Pride Lands into ruin. You failed to keep the lionesses in line. And you failed to kill Simba in the first place, enabling him to return, fully grown, and challenge my rule!

HA HA loohohohoooheeee!

Okay, so, some of that might be true.

That's what *I* thought.

I still feel like if you'd been a better king, none of this would have happened, but . . . whatever.

Hmph. Your idiocy forced me into "early retirement," shall we say? Everything *I* worked for, all my hopes and dreams, shattered. And thus, the Pride Lands lost their greatest and most brilliant ruler.

Cruella De Vil

SKILLS:

- Creating clothing designs for the well-dressed elite
- Fur trading
- Living the good life

EDUCATION:

- Only the best that money could buy, darlings

PRIOR WORK EXPERIENCE:

- Fashion designer
- Socialite
- Heiress

HAIR COLOR:

- Ebony black and ivory white

EYE COLOR:

- Black as the finest mink coat

LIKES:

- Furs (every stripe, spot, and hue)
- High fashion
- High society
- My many vices

DISLIKES:

- Animals (especially dogs)
- Low-class people
- Not getting what I deserve

Curse that Roger and his wretched, wretched song about me! "If she doesn't scare you, no evil thing will?" EVIL INDEED! I can't believe my schoolmate Anita married him. Jasper! Horace!

Y-yes ma'am?

Remind me again about the "EVIL" deeds I've supposedly done?

Well, ma'am, as I recall it, you asked us to go 'round the country buying up all the Dalmatian puppies we could get our hands on.

A bleedin' ton of them there was!

And then you was gonna have us kill 'em and skin 'em for their fur, so's you could make coats and such like.

 BEAUTIFUL COATS. The fur of a Dalmatian is perfectly dazzling, and sewn into coats, it would have been stunning.

And we—

SHUT It, Horace, I'm telling the story. Anyway, just when we had about all the puppies we could handle, you decided that wasn't quite enough, so you had us steal fifteen more from that old school chum of yours. Brought the total to ninety-nine, and brought the law down on us, you did!

Oh, blast it! You idiots have quite missed the point of the whole endeavor. And it's clear you wouldn't know FASHION if it came up and bit you on your horrid noses.

Yes, I told Jasper and Horace to steal the puppies from my old school "friend" Anita and her wretched husband, Roger. And yes, I was going to make coats out of them. But such gorgeous coats.

You see, I LIVE FOR FURS.
I positively worship furs. And every woman of any taste and breeding does too. You should have seen my plans—the coats I made out of those awful mongrels would have been glorious. I would have had the fashion elite of London eating out of my manicured hands.

Certainly some say it's evil to make coats out of dog fur. I say that with fur that beautiful, it would be a greater crime to only let dogs wear it, don't you agree, Jasper?

But no, you two imbeciles let the puppies get away!

Well, ma'am, I —

Oi, now be reasonable, missus, they were bloody clever dogs.

Please, you bumbling fools were outsmarted by a pack of animals, and now my beautiful coats will never be made. You ruined me. Well, you and that awful Roger and his "Cruella De Vil" song. Blast it all. He made me into the laughingstock of the whole country, and you nitwits left me with no recourse to restore my good name.

Well mark my words, when everyone in the country is wearing DeVil brand fur coats, they'll be sorry!
Just you wait and see!

GASTON

PRIOR WORK EXPERIENCE:

- Hunter
- Most popular man in the village
- Handsomest man in the village

EDUCATION:

- Who needs education when you have muscles?

SKILLS:

- Shooting
- Fighting
- Punching
- Eating eggs
- Hunting
- Sword fighting
- Biting
- Growing hair
- Wrestling
- Horseback riding
- Spitting
- Using antlers in decorating
- Really, too many to list

LIKES:

- Hunting things
- Shooting things
- Punching things
- Being admired
- Muscles
- Belle
- Big meals

DISLIKES:

- Books with too many words
- Brainy girls
- Crazy inventors
- Mysterious castles in the woods
- Beasts who are secretly princes

WEAPON OF CHOICE:

- Crossbow

HAIR COLOR:

- Coal black

EYE COLOR:

- Baby blue

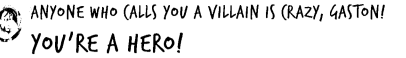

ANYONE WHO CALLS YOU A VILLAIN IS CRAZY, GASTON!

YOU'RE A HERO!

I know, right? The GREATEST HERO *our village—no, all of* France—*has ever known! The only one who thought I was a villain was* Belle *and that crazy father of hers,* Maurice. *I spent my whole life protecting that village and just generally being* THE BEST, *and what thanks do I get?*

A WHOLE LOT OF NOTHIN', THAT'S WHAT!

I was the only one who saw Belle *for the beautiful girl she was. I was even willing to look past all her many, many flaws and ask her to be my wife. I mean, who wants a girl who reads, and thinks for herself?* UGH!

But still, she is beautiful—the most beautiful girl in town. Which makes her the only one worthy of marriage to me. But she had the nerve to turn me down!

 ## THE NERVE!

 Me! Gaston! Again, **BASICALLY THE BEST.** *Do you know how many gorgeous, eligible young ladies throw themselves at me every day? Dozens!*

BAKER'S DOZENS!

I mean, did she think she was going to do better? There is no one better than me! And even after the humiliation of her rejection, I was magnanimous enough to forgive and forget.

 BUT GASTON, I THOUGHT YOU WERE GOING TO FORCE BELLE TO MARRY YOU BY HAVING HER FATHER THROWN IN THE ASYLUM?

 As I said, forgive and forget.

Anyway, I thought Maurice was just a crazy old kook. When he came into the tavern ranting about a castle and a beast and talking furniture—how could any man believe that nonsense? Why, when Belle appeared and started spouting the same silliness, I was prepared to believe that she'd lost her marbles, too! It would certainly explain why she turned down my proposal.

 TRUE.

How was I to know there REALLY was a horrible Beast lurking in a castle in the woods? It's the sort of thing you have to see to believe. And once Belle proved it to me, I took the most reasonable next step.

ORGANIZING AN ANGRY MOB?

PRECISELY.
Belle kept babbling about how he was KIND AND GENTLE. Pah!

When there's a monster out in the world, you don't make friends with it! You certainly don't fall in love with it. You kill it, and you mount its head on your wall!

I gathered every able-bodied man in the village, armed them with torches and pitchforks, and marched on that castle with my makeshift army, just **LIKE ANY HERO WOULD.**

 TOO BAD IT DIDN'T GO SO WELL FOR US, HUH?

Don't be ridiculous, LeFou. It was a perfect success. I defeated that monstrous Beast and married the girl of my dreams. Even now I'm still the most admired man in the village. No, in all of France! No one needs to hear differently.

YOU HAVEN'T HEARD DIFFERENTLY.

HAVE YOU?

SKILLS:

- Curses
- Hypnosis
- Teleportation
- Conjuration
- Metamorphosis
- Evil horticulture

HAIR COLOR:

- Trade secret

EYE COLOR:

- Golden yellow

PRIZED POSSESSION:

- Magical staff

PRIOR WORK EXPERIENCE:

- Wicked Fairy
- Mistress of All Evil
- Ruler of the Forbidden Mountain

EDUCATION:

- When you are an immortal fairy,
  you educate. You are not educated.

LIKES:

- Evil
- Cruelty
- Sorrow
- Revenge
- Unlimited power

DISLIKES:

- Heroic princes
- Disrespect
- Idiotic minions
- Good fairies
- Enchanted swords
- Not being invited to royal celebrations

 **Merely observe my title, and you will know the truth—"Mistress of All Evil." That my deeds are the wickedest is a fact acknowledged far and wide.**

Thus, King Stefan and his queen should have known their great error when they failed to invite me to their daughter's christening. How could I, the most villainous force in the land, possibly stand such an insult?

 **CAW!**

 **Indeed, my pet. And yet they had the gall to invite those foolish, flittering "GOOD FAIRIES." An inexcusable breach of etiquette. What gifts could such weaklings bestow upon Princess Aurora that I could not have outdone tenfold, had I merely been given the chance?**

Why, I could have had rubies spill from her lips when she spoke, or made her powerful enough to call lightning down with a wave of her hand. What little girl wouldn't want that?

But no, I was overlooked. And when I laid a curse upon the infant, I was merely repaying their royal highnesses' rudeness in kind.

My spell intended that upon Aurora's sixteenth birthday, she would prick her finger on the needle of a SPINNING WHEEL . . . and die. A fitting recompense, I felt. But one of the good fairies interfered—softening my curse so that Aurora would merely sleep, awaiting true love's first kiss to awaken her. SUCH A NOVEL SOLUTION.

King Stefan tried to circumvent my curse by ordering all spinning wheels in the kingdom burned, and the "good fairies" hid their precious princess away somewhere, to try to prevent my curse from reaching her. All that their foolishness accomplished was to increase my wrath.

Instead of peacefully accepting their fate, they led me on a sixteen-year wild goose chase. As you can imagine, by the end of the hunt, I was no longer in a merciful mood. Especially once I found that my idiot minions had spent all sixteen years looking for a babe in the cradle. All that time wasted. I saw that they paid for *THAT.*

 # CAW, AWK!

Don't worry, my sweet, I hadn't forgotten about you. Indeed, it was you, my beautiful raven, who finally found the beautiful young maiden secreted away in a humble cottage in the woods. I should have set you on the case to begin with. Those foolish fairies practically led you right to her.

And once I knew where she was, it took mere moments to hypnotize her into pricking her finger and fulfilling my curse. Of course, there was still that little loophole of "TRUE LOVE'S FIRST KISS" to worry about—but as luck would have it, she'd already met her true love, Prince Phillip. All I had to do was imprison him, and the curse would *NEVER* be broken.

Of course, my fairy brethren couldn't leave well enough alone. They had the temerity to release Phillip from my dungeons and arm him with the Sword of Truth, and the Shield of Virtue. My idiot minions could not even stop him from escaping through the gates of my fortress.

To slow down the little princeling from reaching the castle, I called upon my dark powers to cause a forest of thorns to grow up around the castle where his "SLEEPING BEAUTY" lay. I thought surely it would be his end—but even that did not stop him. His blasted Sword of Truth cleaved through my fortifications.

I had to take my most magnificent form in order to prevent my evil schemes from being undone. And I did, of course. The Mistress of All Evil never fails in her grand designs—not even when faced with magic swords and shields and determined princes.

CAW?

Fail? Certainly not. I did not fail. And may I add, I do _NOT_ appreciate your tone, my raven.

QUEEN OF HEARTS

SKILLS:

- Croquet
- Beheading
- Shouting
- Giving orders
- Judging trials

PRIOR WORK EXPERIENCE:

- Ruler of Wonderland

EDUCATION:

- Don't be ridiculous.
  Whoever learned anything in school?

PRIZED POSSESSION:

- Royal rose garden

LIKES:

- Croquet
- Winning
- Being obeyed
- Beheadings
- Red roses

DISLIKES:

- Cheshire cats
- Impudent little girls
- Losing at croquet
- Not getting my way
- White roses

EYE COLOR:

- Black
  Why are they black?
  Paint them red at once!

HAIR COLOR:

- Red—no, I mean, black

OFF WITH THEIR HEADS!! Ah, I mean, guard! Attention!

Yes, Your Majesty!

Am I not the unquestioned ruler of Wonderland?

Yes, Your Majesty!

And as the ruler of Wonderland, can anything I do be called "evil?"

Yes, Your Majesty! We mean, **NO, YOUR MAJESTY!**

PRECISELY! I am the queen, therefore everything I do must be good. Because if it were not good, I would not do it. You see? It is perfectly logical.

Well? Agree with me!!

9

Yes, Your Majesty! Of course, Your Majesty!

Now there are those who say that I am . . . unreasonable. That I am too quick to anger, that I order too many executions, and that I cheat at croquet. Indeed, there are those who would even call me . . . oh, what did that impertinent Alice girl say?

A fat, pompous, bad-tempered old tyrant, Your Majesty?

OFF WITH YOUR HEAD!!

 I was only quoting, Your Majesty!

Oh, were you? Then . . .
OFF WITH HIS HEAD!
What was I saying? Oh yes. The very idea that
I am a ruthless tyrant is patently UNTRUE,
UNFAIR, and UNJUST. And I should know a
thing or two about justice, as not only am I
queen, but I preside over all trials in Wonderland.
All accused who come before me are judged, and
have their heads chopped
off because they are
unquestionably guilty.
Does that sound evil
to you?

NO, YOUR MAJESTY!

SIIIILENCE!!

It must be unquestionably clear to anyone who is paying attention that I am adored and dreaded by my subjects. Is it better to be loved or feared? Was it one or the other or was it both?

You know, it doesn't matter.
I'm the Queen, and what I say goes!
All ways in Wonderland are MY ways!

Yes, Your Majesty!

Exactly. And if anyone says otherwise, OFF WITH THEIR HEADS!

Captain Hook

SKILLS:

- Expert swordsman
- Excellent marksman
- Persuasive negotiator
- Sailing and captaining a sea vessel

PRIOR WORK EXPERIENCE:

- World's most famous crook
- Captain of the *Jolly Roger*

EDUCATION:

- The sea

WEAPON OF CHOICE:

- Sword

LIKES:

- Treasure
- Fairy dust
- Mermaids
- Mr. Smee and a loyal pirate crew

DISLIKES:

- Peter Pan
- The Lost Boys
- Sassy fairies
- Being called "Codfish"
- Alarm clocks
- Crocodiles (especially crocodiles who have swallowed alarm clocks)

HAIR COLOR:

- Black as boot polish

EYE COLOR:

- Brown as driftwood

Smee! Read the list!

The list, Captain?

The list, Smee! The list of me cunning crimes and dastardly deeds! <u>READ IT!</u>

Oh! Yes! Of course, Captain! Let's see here. Piracy, privateering, ship-scuttling, theft, murder, assault, smuggling, extortion, illegal dueling, forgery, sailing under false colors, sailing under true colors, looting, kidnapping, fairy-napping, arson, idleness, and general bad behavior.

 Now those are the actions of a true villain, unmatched in any sphere! No mere scoundrel or scofflaw, I—no, Captain Hook is the blackguard of blackguards! The criminal of criminals! The apex of evildoers! Commanding the roughest crew of scurvy swabbies the seven seas have ever known!

Peter Pan would certainly agree with you, Captain.

Peter Pan? Don't speak that name around me, Smee!

 Oh, I do beg your pardon, Captain.

To think, a magnificent malefactor such as myself, was undone by a mere boy. Do you know how I got this hook?

Yes, Captain. Peter—

Peter Pan lopped my hand off and fed it to a crocodile. The foul beast liked the taste of me so much that he's stalked my every move since, hoping to feast on the rest of me. My only saving grace is that the dumb creature swallowed an alarm clock, so he ticks and tocks wherever he goes. But I, the great Captain Hook, must live my life in terror of that sound! The humiliation of it all!

There, there, Captain.

I could have ruled Neverland long ago, if only that boy didn't shadow my every move. Taunting me, flying through the air just out of reach, calling me a codfish . . . My nerves are shot!

I almost had that blasted boy in me grasp, Smee—when Tinker Bell turned against him. That persnickety pixie showed me where he and the Lost Boys made their home, and that was nearly enough to bring about his end! But once more victory slipped through my grasp.

The things I've seen and done, Smee! They should be writing books about me! But no, they tell tales of that rapscallion, and make me out to be a mere dilettante!

It's only because you're such a gentleman, Captain. Peter Pan just doesn't play fair.

Blast fairness! I want that boy dead, Smee!

 Oh, Captain, I can't help but feel you just ain't your old self anymore. Back when we was living a proper piratical life, we were scuttlin' ships and cuttin' throats and having ourselves a jolly old time. Now it's all Peter Pan this and Peter Pan that—it ain't healthy, Captain!

You want me to leave Neverland?

Yes, Captain! The crew and I have been saying that for years!

Blast it all Smee! We can't possibly leave yet! Not without defeating Pan! After all, how can I call myself the apex of evildoers if I've not yet bested my greatest foe?

Aww, Captain. You're still the most black-hearted, depraved, nefarious pirate on the Seven Seas!

Well, thank you, Smee. You do always know what to say.

HADES

SKILLS:

- Pyromancy
- Transformation
- Teleportation
- Monster summoning

EDUCATION:

- Nada, zip, zilch—self-taught—baby

PRIOR WORK EXPERIENCE:

- Lord of the Dead
- Ruler of the Underworld
- King of Olympus (temporarily)

WEAPON OF CHOICE:

- Other people

EYE COLOR:

- Fiery yellow

HAIR COLOR:

- Flaming blue

LIKES:

- Causing chaos
- Manipulation
- Titans
- Mount Olympus
- Plotting to overthrow Zeus

DISLIKES:

- The Underworld
- Dead people
- Zeus
- Hercules
- Idiot employees
- Love

You want to know my story? Oh-ho, my friends, have I got a story for you.

BUT LORD HADES, WE ALREADY KNOW YOUR—

 Y'see, a long time ago the world was ruled by these giant monsters called Titans. Big, mean, ugly schmucks who would just as soon eat you as look at you. Then this fella named Zeus—my putz of an older brother, just my luck—came along, took one look at them, and said "scram!" He threw a bunch of thunderbolts at them—that's kind of his thing—and locked them all away where they couldn't cause any more problems.

Then he divided the rest of the world up into realms among the other gods. Including me, see, I'm a god, too. But you know what he gives me?

 THE . . . THE UNDERWORLD?

The Underworld, i.e., the DARKEST, DANKEST, GLOOMIEST place on Earth. Or under it. Whatever. The point is, he gives me a full-time job that's literally the bottom of the barrel and expects me to be all "ohhh, thanks big brother, couldn't be happier!" While he parties it up on Mount Olympus with all his god buddies. Puh-leaze.

So I do what anyone would do in that situation. I plot to overthrow my brother. I MEAN, WHAT DID HE EXPECT?

YOU ARE SO RIGHT, YOUR LUGUBRIOUSNESS!

But then a wrench got thrown into my expertly crafted plans. Zeus has a kid. An annoying little sunspot named Hercules. Now, the Fates tell me that this kid spells disaster for me, so I do what I can to mitigate the situation. I tell these two little worms to kidnap the little sunspot and turn him mortal. Then kill him. Simple enough, right? But they can't even do that much.

WE ARE SO, SO SORRY YOUR EVILNESS—

PIPE DOWN. So wonder-brat Hercules is mortal, but he keeps enough of his godly strength to keep being a major pain in my neck. I keep throwing monsters at him left and right, but he brushes them off like it's no big deal. I tell you, I can't win.

Zeus even bends the rules to show some nepotism.
Gets him in with the big-shot hero trainer, Philoctetes.
Where was that family spirit when he was handing out the
almighty assignments, I ask you? This is me, always drawing
the short straw. Oy.

But do I sit around whining? No! I roll with the punches. So Hercules
is good at monsters—I just gotta find his real weakness, right?

Turns out, I had just the thing sitting in my back
pocket. A cute little gal named Megara, who
Jerkules just happened to fall in love with.
So badda boom, I put Meg in mortal peril,
and badda bing, Hercules agrees to give
up his strength for a day. The very day
my big attack was planned to go down.

PROBLEM. SOLVED.

Did I mention I'd released the Titans?

NO, YOUR PERSPICACIOUSNESS!

Right, well, I released the Titans. You remember them. Big, ugly, with the gnashing and the eating and the death and destruction, etcetera? I set 'em loose on Mount Olympus, right when the fates decreed that Zeus would be at his weakest.

But then, get this—Meg has the dumb luck to get crushed under a column. She breaks my deal. So just when I'm about to get everything I wanted, everything I spent millennia planning for, who comes back at full strength to ruin my day?

UM . . . HERCULES?

Of course Hercules, you dumb mook! So I'm back at square one. LOWER THAN SQUARE ONE.

But then I think maybe I can get a little bit of a consolation prize. See, Meg died, so I convinced Mr. Wonderful to trade his life for hers. She comes out of the Underworld, he goes in. But ohhh no, even that backfires, because it turns out sacrificing himself is enough to tip the scales and get the mighty Hercules his immortality back.

Story of my life, everyone gets a happy ending except me. I'm stuck down here in the Underworld for the foreseeable *FOREVER.*

Of course, Hercules turned down his chance to be a god to stay mortal, so . . . well, let's just say I'll be seeing him again someday.

SKILLS:

- Voodoo
- Magic potions and powders
- Tarot and palm reading
- Curses
- Transmogrification

PRIZED POSSESSION:

- Deck of cards

EDUCATION:

- Taught voodoo magic by "friends" on the Other Side

PRIOR WORK EXPERIENCE:

- Swindler
- Card sharp
- Witch doctor
- Fortune teller
- Owner and proprietor of Dr. Facilier's Voodoo Emporium

LIKES:

- Riches
- Power
- Voodoo magic
- Being on top

DISLIKES:

- Magical debts
- Being poor
- Disrespect
- Wealthy folks

HAIR COLOR:

- Dark as black magic

EYE COLOR:

- Nightshade violet

I'M A FORTUNE TELLER BY TRADE, AND I CAN SEE YOUR FUTURE AS CLEAR AS DAY. I SEE YOU : . . BEING FASCINATED BY MY TALE! **YES, YOU!**

???
. . .

QUIET, YOU, IT'S GOOD PRACTICE FOR THE SUCKERS.

NOW I MAKE MY HOME IN NEW ORLEANS, A HUSTLING, BUSTLING CITY—AND LET ME TELL YOU, NO ONE HUSTLES MORE THAN DR. FACILIER. BUT IN THIS CITY WHERE RICH AND POOR RUB ELBOWS ON THE TROLLEY, IT'S HARD NOT TO FEEL LET DOWN WHEN YOU'RE ONE OF THE LATTER.

ME, I HAD PLANS TO RISE ABOVE MY STATION—AND I SAW MY BEST SHOT AT A MEAL TICKET ARRIVE ON THE RIVER BOAT IN THE FORM OF ONE PRINCE NAVEEN OF MALDONIA. HIS FLASHY PLAYBOY LIFESTYLE HAD HIS PARENTS DISGRUNTLED AND HIS MANSERVANT LAWRENCE MORE THAN WILLING TO DO A DEAL WITH **THE SHADOW MAN. . . .** THAT'D BE ME.

!!!
. . .

YES, AND YOU.

 **One handshake deal later and Lawrence was looking and living the lavish lifestyle to which I hoped to become accustomed, and Prince Naveen was . . . well, he was feeling a little GREEN around the gills.**

We were gonna keep the ruse up long enough for Lawrence to get hitched to a pretty, rich young thing and get a handsome payout— which he'd split with me, of course, seeing as how I was matchmaker to this little arrangement.

BUT THEN WHAT HAPPENS? HE LOSES OUR FROGGY PRISONER, AND MY "FRIENDS" ON THE OTHER SIDE GET A MITE . . . ANTSY. I HAVE TO MAKE A FEW EXTRA PROMISES TO TRY TO GET THE PRINCE BACK SAFELY, PROMISES I WASN'T TOO HAPPY ABOUT MAKING. WHEN YOU DEAL WITH VOODOO, SOMETIMES WHAT THEY TAKE IS MORE THAN WHAT YOU CAN AFFORD, IF YOU KNOW WHAT I'M SAYING.

I SEND SHADOWS AND SHADES OUT INTO EVERY CORNER OF THE BAYOU. HAVE YOU EVER TRIED HUNTING FOR A FROG IN THE BAYOU? LIKE HUNTING FOR A NEEDLE IN A HAYSTACK MADE OUT OF NEEDLES. BUT I FIND HIM, BECAUSE I'M THE BEST THERE IS, MY FRIEND.

THEN THIS MEDDLING WAITRESS NAMED TIANA GOT IN MY WAY. NO "TRUE LOVE'S FIRST KISS" COULD BREAK THE SPELL I COOKED UP, BUT SHE STILL MANAGED TO RUIN MY PLANS.

AND THAT'S DESPITE ME BEING MY MOST GENEROUS SELF AND OFFERING HER HEART'S DESIRE TO HER ON A SILVER PLATTER.

She'd **NEVER** find a better bargain than the one I offered her. But she wouldn't take it—and she got me in some mighty hot water with my "friends."

You know what voodoo do when you're on its **BAD** side?

● ???!!!

Actually, you know what—you don't want to know. Just trust me when I say it ain't pretty. But the Big Easy hasn't seen the last of Dr. Facilier! Sure as a bad penny keeps turning up... **I'll be back.**

DISNEY

VILLAINS

Studio Fun International
An imprint of Printers Row Publishing Group
A division of Readerlink Distribution Services, LLC
10350 Barnes Canyon Road, Suite 100, San Diego, CA 92121
www.studiofun.com

Written by Rachael Upton
Cover illustrated by The Disney Book Group
Interior art by Luigi Aime, Franck Broquet, and The Disney Book Group
Designed by Kara Kenna and Mariel Lopez-Cotero

Studio Fun International is a registered trademark of Readerlink Distribution Services, LLC.
All notations of errors or omissions should be addressed to Studio Fun International,
Editorial Department, at the above address.

ISBN: 978-0-7944-4160-9

Manufactured, printed, and assembled in Shaoguan, China. SL/05/18
22 21 20 19 18 2 3 4 5 6